Liberation Now!

Liberation Now!

5 STEPS TO BEGIN REALIZING YOUR DREAMS

Tamara L. McMillan

To order additional copies of this book, contact:
Xlibris
1-888-795-4274
www.Xlibris.com
Orders@Xlibris.com
773268

CONTENTS

THIS BOOK IS dedicated to three of the most essential, unrelenting and forgiving influences in my life. First, it's because the universe created, molded and poured into me all the things that would make projects like this book possible…I humbly stand in my authenticity with an unapologetic and brave stance.

To my younger self, I am forever indebted to you. As you're the true hero in all of this. You stood in the gap, most times insecure, unknowing and feeling like a misfit. Your bravery and willingness to continue moving forward has not gone unnoticed or unappreciated. Thank you for holding the baton of guilt, shame and brokenness without a fault so that I may live a life of abundance.

Last, but certainly not least…to my daughter. The sharper, more beautiful and bolder version of myself. You are truly the dopest daughter a mother could have asked for. Your keen awareness of self, guts and perseverance to do things on your own terms is exhilarating. I thank you for allowing me to come along for the ride. A window seat into your world is majestic and royal just like you. You are my first real love and most importantly…you represent the best thing that has ever happened to me. For this, I thank you with all that I am.

ACKNOWLEDGMENTS

THERE ARE TRULY so many people to acknowledge and thank you as the support of my growth and life as a practicing practitioner of my art has been endless. I will do my best to capture everyone on this small page, however, I realize the feat will be difficult. So, here is my best attempt for this book. In no particular order:

- My sisters, TRM and TLV, both of you have helped to nurture not only my dreams but also JDW. We have shared many things from growing up in the projects to graduating college a few times, marriages, a few divorces, kids, buying homes and a few disagreements. However, the one thing that has remained a constant is our support, appreciation and undying love for one another. The intimacy shared between us is irrefutable. Know that I am nothing without both of you.

- My BFF, anyone who knows me, knows that I have one BFF that has been there with me since high school as a LaFayette violet. WLM, we have seen a lot, celebrated many birthdays and cried a river once or twice. Gurl, thanks for being the ultimate side-kick, homegirl, sounding board, and best friend in the whole wide world.

- The Krew, you know who you are. I have the pleasure of being associated with the best Sorority for me and thus I have gained many more sisters. Ladies, I love our outings, birthday celebrations, anniversaries and the times when we're just chilling having great laughs.

- The Tribe: From making sure that my presentations are picture perfect on paper, to recording and posting videos of me in action on social media to ensuring that I own the room once I walk out on stage, I know my back is covered. It's an amazing feeling being connected to the badest tribe in the land.

- Scholars, I have had the awesome pleasure of sitting at your feet in and outside of the classroom. Thank you for embracing our unorthodox, organic and natural environment where everyone is afforded a seat at the table. Thanks for following, supporting, encouraging, and loving MEE unconditionally. I look forward to our continued growth.

- The Board: To all of the brilliant, beautiful and caring women who sat on the board at one time or another. I thank you for sharing your time, talents and treasurers as we attempt to raise the consciousness of those we come in contact with via our programming, events, conferences and roundtable discussions.

- Artisan Journey, thanks for lending a hand with editing when you could. I appreciate you taking the time to support this project.

- P.I.G., my performance coach, man who knew? Unmistakably, you have this elegant and savvy approach of presenting life that makes everyone you come in contact with stop, listen and ponder. Your acumen for threading the needle in a way that bring your clients along is exacting. Luminous you are for sure. I thank you for honoring my being by awakening the Goddess within MEE!

- My Mother, you are my first and best example of black feminism. The seamless way you loved my sisters and

I equally while balancing our stark personalities. You held us up while also holding us accountable. Forced into a life you didn't want, not only did you rise to the occasion you left a lite trail for us to follow. All that I am or hope to be, I owe to you.

I T'S WITH ENORMOUS gratitude, emotion and a heavy heart that I thank you for purchasing this book and making the decision to take this journey with MEE. There are a plethora of reasons why this book was created. Like all great things are created twice, once in our minds and then on paper, this book is no exception. It's my hope that this book will serve as your invitation or alarm to begin reclaiming your life by incorporating these five steps for realizing your wildest dreams. I don't know about you, but I suffered in silence in almost every area of my life. I was unhappy with my personal, professional, spiritual and emotional lives. I was under the notion that some large hand in the sky would eventually reach down and puck me out of a crowd of over 350 million Americans.

Well, beautiful I wish I could say that's exactly what happened. It wasn't until I began taking responsibility for the things I wanted to change in my life that I noticed a difference. I could see the outlining of something special, as if a switch was initiated on my behalf. I became more conscious of my surroundings, those that occupied my space and the whispers from the universe turned into screams. Finally, with enough strength, courage and confidence I took the bull by the horns. It was simple but there was nothing static about how I began realizing my dreams. You see, the process is continuous even to this today as I'm required to do things that are unthinkable. The pokes to move away from old habits that serve no purpose was blaring. Living a life worth mentioning also required that I move in new circles, circles where I wasn't the only entreprenuer or risk taker in the group. Being comfortable with being uncomfortable was the phrase that paid. As comfort is good but nothing ever grows there.

So, in essence I stopped waiting for someone to pick MEE and I picked my damn self. It was time to get busy living the life I deserved, wanted and of course dreamt of.

~TLM

LIKE THE OLD adage goes, there's nothing new under the sun. These steps, words, ideas and suggestions have been seen, heard and or experienced before. What's different is these concepts are infused, laced and filled with fabric from my personal life. The words that follow are a framework for you to use as a guide to place your unique fabric on as you move through the journey.

This book is accessible. Meaning, it was written with you in mind, as I realize you have multiple demands on your time. Our get it quick, microwave and instant gratification society has made way for platforms like social media, DIY videos and audible to thrive. With this in mind, I didn't say I want this book to be 217 pages, rather I approached this project as a masterpiece of minimalism. A succinct book that gets right to the essence of each step while wrapped with real life examples that could be used as teaching moments.

The caveat…these five steps aren't ALL of the things I did in order to realize my dreams. There were other aspects that

I incorporated in addition to these steps. However, these five steps represent the core grounding of my liberation and the reason why I love my life! The other thing to consider, like anything else in life you will get out of this book what you put into it. If you take this journey seriously; then you will be taken seriously.

Lastly, I love books, as they're magnificent instruments of hope, change, adventure and opportunity. Use this one daily by writing in it, highlight areas that sparkle at you and most importantly break the spine. As this is a true indication that you have immersed yourself in the content.

With all that I am, I wish you all the best that the universe has in store. May your cup runneth over as your hands and heart are filled with an unfailing supply of abundance. Enjoy and allow yourself to experience the full range of emotions.

Lastly, this book isn't perfect as I, the author is imperfect. As a creative I welcome mis-steps and I'm certain you will find a few within these pages. As my mis-steps can be plentiful and specular.

However, the thing I would love for you to concentrate on is taking these steps and making them your own. In the hopes that they inspire you to write your own book, start that business, leave that relationship that isn't working or just decide that you are enough. This book is just now hitting your hands because I was afraid of having my work judged for not being perfect. I'm over it!

Thanks again and prepare to experience your wildest dreams.

TAMARA L. MCMILLAN is an author and award-winning Lecturer at the International Center for Studies in Creativity at SUNY Buffalo State College. Additionally, she consults as a trainer and facilitator in creativity, leadership development, diversity, retention and empowerment. She is qualified in the Myers-Briggs Type Indicator, Strong Interest Inventory, FourSight, and The 7 Habits of Highly Effective People. Tamara designs and delivers workshops in the above areas for the public and private sectors, educators, students and the business community.

She teaches four courses; one in the nature and nurture of Creativity and Disruptive Change Leadership, Creative Approaches to Facilitation, Women and Gender Studies and another in mastering the academic environment. As a speaker and consultant, she provides workshops, presentations, keynotes and training events for such organizations as NYiT, CUNY City College, The Council's Union and Student Programs, Green River College, Kennesaw State University,

University of the Virgin Islands, University at Buffalo, Soledad O'Brien's PowHERful Summit, National Conference for College Women Student Leaders (NCCWSL), LEAD365, Harford Community College, Iowa State University, Alpha Kappa Alpha Sorority, Inc., Workplace Options, Department of Labor (Hamburg, NY), Medaille College, North Carolina A&T and Colleges in the SUNY system. Other clients have included Steve Tasker Self-Leadership Experience camp, Dress for Success Erie and Child and Family Services of Erie County.

Known for her presence, she was one of ten speakers for the inaugural TED conference held in Buffalo, New York in December 2012. She was also a contributing writer for an online magazine that highlights, supports and empowers women. *Stilettos on the Glass Ceiling* has been named top 100 best career websites by Forbes magazine in 2013. Tamara offered guidance and suggestions under the Career column.

Tamara's background is diverse. She has been an associate director for leadership, pharmaceutical senior sales executive, advertising agent, HP and Sun UNIX sales representative, and student employment coordinator. In her spare time, she likes to read, journal and travel.

She is a proud member of Alpha Kappa Alpha Sorority, Inc. and United State of Women. She holds a Bachelor of Science and Master of Science degrees both from SUNY Buffalo State College. Additionally, she holds a certificate of advance studies in Creativity and Change Leadership from the International Center for Studies in Creativity at SUNY Buffalo State College. She's also a doctoral candidate in the Educational Leadership Policies program at the University at Buffalo. Tamara and her daughter, Jontay Deaira resides in Buffalo, New York.

Temet Nosce

You become what you believe

-Oprah Winfrey

THIS BOOK STARTED off in a few different versions of how I thought I wanted it to be presented. I wrestled with myself about which chapter titles would be best, how many words should be in the book. I even went as far as designing an algorithm that would be the lay out for each and every one of my books no matter the content or the constituent. It went something like this, each book would have 7 chapters, and there would be 300 words on each page, 26 pages per chapter which would equate to a 184-188-page book give or take a few pages.

Some of you might be saying to yourself, wow, this is a really dope way to approach writing my book. Yeah, this could be the case. However, for me, deep down inside I knew there was something missing. There was this unshakeable feeling I was unable to dismiss. It wasn't until I thought I had the book layout complete. As each step (no chapters) would be designed the same for uniformity. The quotes would be in the same spot, the affirmation and denial pages would be at the end of each step and all would be dynamic. You see, this just isn't a damn book y'all, the words that you're reading across these white-ish colored pages represent aspects of my life. So, I was stressing myself out about getting it right. Then, during one of my sessions with my performance coach, I asked him to assist with teasing out the minutiae for one concept. Before I could begin explaining the concept I needed his brain for, quite simply, he asked "what do you want your readers to walk away knowing?" I replied with a smug look on my face, I want for them what I want for myself…a deeper sense of self, heightened level of consciousness and for them to know their dreams are worth following. Ok, he said showing those beautiful pearly whites. Then I knew it, he was going in for the kill. His brilliance always come in the room before he does. Then he said sweetly, "give them you"!

 TAMARA L. MCMILLAN

It was like that silver bullet crossing into the umber grey sky with a red line. It was my "a ha" moment if you will. What was missing from what I had started with the first few steps and the well-designed outline was…myself. I was so concerned yet again with getting this shit right, that I had a lapse in judgement and left my creative consultant hat on the side of my desk. As a creative we live for the opportunities to make mistakes, get things wrong and doing it with confidence and style. This is one of the many reasons why I titled the first step in Latin; "Temet Nosce" means "Thyself, thou must know". This quote by Socrates has been used in many books, movies and classrooms globally. I believe there's no way for anyone of us to accomplish our purest dreams without fully understanding self. The struggle to get the right voice, angle and perspective was arduous because I wasn't being true to my game.

Uggggh, this is why I love my life. For those of you who follow me on IG, that's Instagram for people like my mother and grandmother who will read this and say "what the hell is IG"? Well, okay, maybe not my grandmother but definitely my mother. L-boogie is hilarious and she was my first example of a real black feminist. More on my mother is soon to come. As

I digress, on social media I started a #Ilovemylife campaign. Here is where I allowed my faithful 5k plus followers to come along for the ride. I shared events, feelings and things that are important to me via pictures and captions underneath that showed how I was winning in many aspects. Now, please don't get it twisted, just because I had this campaign doesn't mean I had been exempt from trials and challenges. Gurl, please, not at all under any circumstances. Life for me ain't been no walk in the park as I often now tell anyone who will listen. This brave title adapted from the famous Langston Hughes's poem really sums up my life. Especially my earlier years, growing up in a single parent home on the east side of Buffalo, New York. Kenfield-Langfield is where I spent most of days, but I wasn't out chilling nor relaxing. As there's nothing relaxing about growing up in the projects on welfare. There were many struggles we had to endure and overcome as a tribe of four. My mother of course leading the helm, wasn't quite sure on how to manage our new landscape. Growing up under the tutelage of a strong and unrelenting black woman, I was scared to death of everything to include her. My mother didn't consciously choose the position of feminist, rather her divorce from my father thrusted her into prime time. Where

TAMARA L. MCMILLAN

the black feminist movement was taking shape. Shirley Chisholm had just been elected as the first black woman into the US Congress a few years prior in 1969. Then off the heels of this monumental feat, three years later in 1972, Angela Y. Davis was acquitted on charges of conspiracy, murder and kidnapping. All taking place one to two years after the finalization of my parents' divorce and my father's decision to start a new life with a new wife and daughter in Hot-lanta.

But before our world was turned upside down, my introduction into the family was met with much fanfare and anticipation. I was the first child, first grandchild on my mother's side and the first granddaughter on my father's. I think this could be the reason why I like being first? To say that I was spoiled would be a gross understatement. My parents adored me and so did my grandparents, aunts and uncles. I often recall them telling me numerous times how my mother was adamant about all things concerning me.

She was very particular about who I stayed with and what I wore. I understand that I had all the cutest dresses a little girl could want. For me, the unfortunate thing is my mother had very few pictures of her and I. Being the oldest lass, I was expecting to have more pictures that represented our short two years alone. I'm not certain if our pictures were lost in the haste to move from our house on Edna Street. Was the pain of having her heart broken and the brevity of being the custodial parent for three little girls enough to leave everything behind? To this day, I only have two pictures of my mother and me when I was younger. Whenever I come across these pictures, I find myself staring at them in amazement and admiration.

The pictures represent a bond that at times can't be explained and a mutual support between a mother and her daughter. In the one photo, my mother was seated and with one of her arms holding me up as I attempted to walk. I know that I'm not there yet, as I'm stylishly wearing those hideous white baby walking shoes. However, I must say she did an awesome job of putting me together. As I looked stinkin cute in my blue swing dress with the white lace collar.

From the very beginning I knew I was different. I remember never fitting in but feeling comfortable in surroundings where I could demonstrate my speaking prowess. You see growing up in the projects wasn't all that bad. Of course, there were many challenges, struggles and lack of almost anything you could imagine. My sisters and I slept on beds that were passed down from our aunts, when our grandmother purchased new

TAMARA L. MCMILLAN

ones for them. Sleeping in one bedroom in the beginning was pretty cool. We were best friends, we kept each other company and we often got into mischief together. Who better than your sisters to get into trouble with and suffer the same punishment. I recall one of the most horrifying times when our mother was totally outdone with us. We were in our little room with a full-sized bed along one wall and a twin along the other. One of us suggested that we try our hands at being the next Jean-Michel Basquiat or Picasso. What better canvas than the clean white wall we saw picture less every day. Therefore, we took to expressing our creativity. We laughed, giggled and pointed at each other's work in esteem and zeal. The carefree moment took a turn when one sister wasn't given enough space on our free tarp to continue creating with our mostly broken crayons. As a result, down the stairs she went moving with precision to gain the support of our mother. Confused about what was going on, she came upstairs to feed her curiosity and to take a glance. What she saw immediately sent her over the fucking edge. The words from her mouth sprayed the room like venom. The flow was effortless like the artistry of a spoken word poet, we were shook down to our socks. To say she handled the situation would be an understatement. My mother did her best to understand our naïve perspective. My sisters and I often laugh about our upbringing, reminiscing on the crazy things we did and our colossal come up in the world. In lieu of the many hardships there were numerous happy times in our tiny apartment. Our mother wasn't by far perfect, but all three of us would agree collectively she was perfect for us! Sure, I would have loved more resources growing up, but she made certain we had the necessities to be our best. The thought of her deep and raspy voice caught my attention instantly. She spoke with such command that it was both electrifying yet intimidating for a young vulnerable me.

Maybe this is why I love the English language and the way words roll off of my tongue when speaking. I watched the way she maneuvered her conversations, especially the ones I wanted to be a part of. I remember coming home from a field trip in the 8th grade. We went to Darien Lake for our class trip to end the academic year. I felt alone as I caught the bus home from school. My classmates who also lived in the projects with me were on the bus. However, they all seemed to be in their own world. They were laughing, recalling the events from our trip and in a happy trance. They presented themselves as if they had no worries in the world. They chuckled and smirked as if we were on our way to some posh cribs located deep in a cul-de-sac. After catching two buses to get home, dejected and mentally exhausted, I walked into the back circle parking lot that lead to our back door along with at least 20 other families. It was a beautiful day in June, the sun was unrelenting and the sky was clear. As I meandered through the court and approached the walk-way that we shared with Ms. Anne and her family. I could see both ladies sitting under the large oak tree at the foot of the walk-way next to the parking area. They both said hello and I responded with a dry hi. Noticing there was something off in my demeanor, my mother asked "what's wrong"? I replied nothing and to my miscalculation she said ok. Devastated, I thought to myself… really? She couldn't be serious; how did she not know that I needed her to ask me again. I needed her to exercise better judgement and tap into her emotional intelligence. This was another epic fail and a missed opportunity for her and I to create a more fluid relationship. As I began leaning more into who I was, I uncovered that open, honest and judgement free dialogues were an essential part of my growth. As a creative I needed a space where my voice and opinions could be heard and valued no matter the subject. My mother for the most part ran a diplomatic household, however, there were some things that weren't up for discussion. This along with appreciating my so-called friendships more than I honored myself created a passive-aggressive attitude. Instead of owning my position, good, bad or indifferent, I would get an attitude and pretend like nothing was wrong.

This kind of self-awareness eventually afforded me the space to better understand her while not betraying me. As self-betrayal to me is the worst kind of betrayal one can experience. I was better able to comprehend her parental platform as a young mother and how she gave what she had in those moments. As we often parent based on the examples given to us. She did the very best she could with what she had, especially after my father left her high and dry…literally! Raising three girls without the support of a father weighed on us all. She could navigate our barrage of questions about him when we were younger. At any rate, as we matured socially and chronologically, the familiarity of his absence was a constant elephant in the room. I believe the attempts to discern how we truly felt about his lack of involvement were at times taxing. So much so, his name came up less and less the older we got. The only times we would see him were on his quick dashes in and out of town. Which meant we had to go over his sister's house in order to see him and play with our cousins. Which equated to us barely spending any quality time with him alone. What a fucking waste of time, energy and hoping, so eventually it didn't matter if we saw him at all. Years would come and go when we wouldn't see and or speak to him. Looking back on this one complexed and fractured aspect of my life, I realized that I suppressed memories that deserved my rescue. Another example of my passive-aggressive trait that I wouldn't fully accept until recently.

The older we got, the more our unique perspectives developed and then disagreements and fights presented themselves. Three young girls living in the same two bedroom apartment with only a living room and kitchen offered no additional space for nothing outside of the normal and we could forget any kind of privacy. There was no place to go and sit, be quite and just reflect. Especially since my mother didn't begin working until I was in junior high school. Someone was always at 7 Kenfield Court. The once large apartment was quickly becoming smaller and smaller. Although we didn't have the latest styles and most expensive clothes and shoes. But when you multiple what we did have times three, things got crowded and messy fast. My dresser drawer was in the hallway situated next to our one bathroom. As our small room wasn't constructed to outfit three growing girls until their late teen years. I cautiously tried not to be too different from the kids I went to school with since I was totally different from the project kids. I dangerously wanted to be a part of the in-crowd which required a certain social status and swag. So, when I began working at the tender age of 16 in the summers, I spent every dime on clothes. I recall spending one complete check at the mall on gear and only had bus fare left. It wasn't until much later in life, that I could see how my deficit mindset was infused in almost every aspect of my existence. It followed me to school, work, with friends and it was definitely visible at home. I remember our refrigerator had no handle and was decorated with a metallic silver and white contact paper. We had to strategically place our fingers in the door-jam to open it. When we wanted to make an ice cream float on Friday nights to watch Dallas. We had to take the ice cream out of the freezer at least ten to fifteen minutes before the show started, as the ice cream would be rock hard due to our freezer over freezing everything. Every so often, we were tasked with unthawing the freezer as the ice build-up would overtake the square space leaving very little room for food. Our family wasn't the only ones that had appliance issues. One of my friend's refrigerator was kept closed by placing a sewing machine in front of it. Many of the families we grew up with lamented some of the same misfortunes.

On the other hand, the one thing that seemed to be present to some degree was a sense of community. The majority of the households in both the Kenfield and Langfield projects were headed by women of color. There were some non-minority families living in the same impoverished conditions just like everyone else. Ms. Anne and her family lived next to us until we moved out at the beginning of my freshmen year in college. There were four kids, her and her live-in boyfriend, who was the father of the youngest. Like the majority of the women heading these households, very few were married. Ms. Anne and my mother were tight. Her boyfriend, Andy was very fond of my mother. Ms. Anne didn't drive, so when she needed to go shopping and he wasn't in the mood he would let my mother drive his car. This was a great benefit for us, as sometimes we got to go and more importantly, my mother could also do some shopping while out. We didn't have a car and were forced to rely on public transportation or my grandmother's car when we had medical appointments. Otherwise, we were on the bus getting from school to home to work and all places in between.

Many of the mothers in our village would keep an eye out for kids other than their own. The lioness for the most part were friendly, strong, and created the best home they could living off of public assistance or low paying jobs. They would get together on the weekends to have card parties, play music, drink and keep one another company. Although close, not all of the women shared the same outlook as my mother. My mother didn't earn her degree until we were older, but she always carried a certain air about her. She carried an attitude that was regal and this was one of the many things I adored about this woman. Gorgeous, with the longest stride that could match any man's walk on his best day, she was the shit even as a project queen. Now, maybe because she's my mother, I believe she's one of the most beautiful women I know to date. A tough cookie and someone you don't want to play with. Her rules were her rules and there was nothing to discuss. This made it difficult to get to know her, especially in the area of relationships. After my father she mustered

 TAMARA L. MCMILLAN

enough strength and courage to seriously date once. This relationship lasted longer than her marriage to my father. He was the first man I saw wear a pair of clogs and made it look sexy as hell. He was dope before we were using the word, his swag was always on point. A classic man, someone that loved music, sports and chips ahoy cookies. He was the closest we got to having a father figure around us. The support my sister's and I received from him was greatly appreciated. My father apparently pulled many disappearing acts. My sister just informed me recently, that he never met my maternal grandfather. I swear I found this extremely ridiculous, how in the hell did he think this was cool? Ok, I'm way off track with what I'm supposed to be sharing. My father's foolishness and buffoonery continues to pull me into another direction. Back to my mother and her finding someone that could care and love her in the way she deserved to be treated. Even though it appeared that love escaped her, figuratively speaking she was confident in her role as our provider. My sisters and I didn't have many things but the one thing we had an abundance of was her love. Now don't misunderstand what I mean by this. For those that know my mother, you know she wasn't and still isn't that emotional warm and fuzzy type of mother who bakes cookies and babysits. In spite of that, there was no doubt in our minds that she would give her very last to ensure her daughters had more than she did. She projected what our lives could be, if we took ourselves seriously. She spoke frankly about aspects of growing up poor and ways we could avoid the perils that impacted many of our friends. It was known in the neighborhood that my mother was mean as a result many of my friends reluctantly came by or called the house. At the time, I was unable to fully comprehend the game she was giving up. But true to form, her words eventually came into fruition.

It wasn't until our different stories began to reveal themselves and still everything didn't make sense then…but it does now! I have friends that I grew up with who still live in those same projects. They have several children, spotty work experience and no real dreams or aspirations worth following. No judgement there, as a matter of fact I feel compassion for them. When you haven't connected with who you are and what your individual purpose is in life…it's easy to get stuck. Many people remain comfortable as they don't know their own potential. They have no idea of what's inside them and how great they are. Self-awareness and acceptance is the

     TAMARA L. MCMILLAN

cornerstone to personal freedom. This is partly why I don't feel sorry for my childhood friends. As we all have the last freedom in the world and that's the freedom to decide! This step is so important because we get to choose what we want in life. The freedom to choose is within all of us. Even in personal misery and lack of resources, I can say confidently, my mother didn't have nor carried a spirit of brokenness. Even when she had no actual money in her purse. She understood there were other kinds of capital. The kind of capital that could lead to money. She channeled the ideology of human capital. She often told my sisters and I, we could be anything we wanted if we were willing to do the work. An educator at heart, she understood that knowledge was the great equalizer. Once she made the decision to get her degree, it was over. Her mindset embraced yet another shift. Her focus was laser sharp and the spirit of abundance began to permeate our lives. For this, I thank her greatly, as she was so convincing in her words, I ultimately believed her. It wouldn't be until I had my daughter that I truly began to understand her plight as a divorcee.

When thinking, processing and embracing how I got to be who I am. I'm left feeling an overwhelming calm. As all of the experiences, especially the fights that I didn't want to be a part of, as I was scared to lose and would rather acquiesce. I desperately needed to be a part of something bigger than myself and that was omnipresent. This thought reminds me of a sleep over I attended, with so-called friends of mine. I was a pre-teen and remember being in the bed after the party ended. Then it started, the teasing, calling me names and bullying. I was made fun of because of who I didn't like. The birthday girl's cousin liked me and she took it personal that I didn't feel the same. The next thing I knew the verbal bullying became physical. As two of the girls began kicking me as they laughed and tormented me for what seemed like hours. I cried myself to sleep and couldn't wait to get home to see my mother.

First off, please know that I would have never told my mother about being bullied at the sleep over. My mother was that chick… she would turn the whole projects out if anyone messed with her kids. She was a fighter and there was no mistaking it. Me, on the other hand, I was a scrawny push over. I would rather dialogue about how fighting solved nothing and it wasn't the right thing to do as humans. You

   TAMARA L. MCMILLAN

against me to knock my panties down. I was out matched and completely out of my damn league. I had no business in any relationship as I didn't have the tools to cope. There was little to no primary criteria for me to use as a guide.

I wouldn't dare stand up for myself, even when I was right. Being betrayed was a common occurrence and I was unsure of how to get off the ride. I remember girls calling my mother's house talking about kicking my ass over a guy I was dating. Not to mention the time I went by a guy's house to chill and watch tv. All of a sudden there was someone banging on the door, come to find out this nigga had a girlfriend and wanted me to hide in his dirty basement. The embarrassment was so great, I was like hell no and this was one of the few times I would have welcomed an ass-kicking. He asked me to stand in the hallway as he ushered her in the front door and asked that I leave out the side once she was in the house. Walking down that driveway was one of the lowest points in my dating career. I use the term "career" loosely as I wasn't learning fast enough through the journey. But as my fate would have it, thankfully, I'm here to proclaim that this isn't the case any longer. Today, I not only stand up for myself, I stand for the voiceless. I remember the beginning of my metamorphosis.

If I felt like someone was trying to control or undermine my personhood. It instantly sent me into attack mode. I could be that angry black bitch when pushed. I'm ok with being called angry when appropriate, if I'm angry, there's a good reason for me to be in that frame of mind. I don't allow myself to get angry often, as it takes up too much emotional and mental space and it's too costly.

The new and improved me does her best to be an example and not a warning for all females not just my daughter. I urge them to stop allowing others to validate their existence. I tell them they are enough and each of them have something special to share with the world. And the only way to do it successfully is by mastering themselves. Doing the hard work first, asking the arduous questions and accepting failure as their pillars and not scars. Posing as the damsel in distress isn't the answer, especially for women of color. The game wasn't written for us and this approach is playing right along into the hands of our patriotic and capitalist society. As women, we don't need someone to pick us, we can pick ourselves. Time magazine named the #metoo movement, person of the year. The photo captured five bad-ass women in all black known as the silence breakers. A movement dedicated to standing up against the injustices that women face at the hands of men. Merriam-Webster also listed "feminism" as the word of the year. As a woman and a feminist, this is a miraculously time to be a female, the playing fields are leveling out. Instead of stating what we don't have as women, let's discuss what is available. Hell, like Shirley Chisolm said if you want a seat at the table bring your own chair.

I've come to appreciate eating alone as I know what I bring to the table. Now, I'm someone who isn't afraid of being vulnerable. As women we ask questions that we already have the answers to. I figured instead of being concerned that my daughter might fall for a controlling and insecure man like I did. I would continue pouring into her, by illustrating her worth and reminding her that she's more than enough. That her value and existence in this world isn't tied to a job or a man for that matter. As a woman I don't want her to concentrate or begin fantasizing about the ideal marriage situation. Like many of my friends and I, we spent too much time on things that really didn't matter, when what we should have been doing is enjoying the roller coaster. Smelling the flowers as we walked by and not jumping at every Tom, Dick and Harry as if they could manage our invisible crowns. I have a plethora of mantra's and one of them reads, if it's for me, then it's for me and only me. Mastering myself took time, it's an active process and there's nothing passive about it. Deconstructing demeaning ideas and ideals was grueling. I was forced to call upon the young me, the girl that had comprehension and reading challenges until high school. The girl who towered over her classmates and had to repeat the second grade. That sweet and noncombative soul who held the torch alone so that I could survive…I owe her everything. As I continue charting the territory on this hero's journey, there's no doubt in my mind that she's the real champion in this story of liberation. As I emerge from the dark corridor having wrestled with my deepest pains, struggles and triumphs. I'm certain this will not be the last trip into that stratosphere. Traumatically, I have come to realize and accept fully that my once dark place will serve as a source of light, enlightenment and self-acceptance for those those around me.

There were no quick fixes during my journey of awareness. I had to begin paying more attention to the subtle cues in my life. Slowing down has been extremely difficult but I have gotten better. Mastering myself is a work of patience, diligence and art. Which helped me realize it wasn't necessary

 TAMARA L. MCMILLAN

to abandon all the things in my past. I could bring forward things like burning incense in my house which my mother did daily. I could announce with pride that I'm from the east side of Buffalo instead of saying Western New York when asked. And finally, I can now celebrate me unapologetically because I am a project girl.

Every adversity, every failure, every heartache carries with it the seed of an equal or greater benefit
-N. Hill

Growth-Mindset

All our dreams can come true-if we have
the courage to pursue them.
-Walt Disney

LIFE FOR ME ain't been no crystal stair. My life story as you've read some of in step 1, has been filled with traumatic events, heartache, pain and lots of struggle. As a tall-skinny awkward project girl, I was forced to grow out of the dirt and concrete. In the beginning, I never felt like I was enough, I was always thinking of ways to escape the land of misfits. I wanted to be teleported to a secret location that was welcoming of individuals like me. For the weary and tired that suffer from a deficit way of thinking. I was defeated before I entered the ring. Unsure of whether I could march on, I for some odd reason just held on for dear life. I capitulated on sight without even processing what mattered to me as I didn't value my worth. To put it plainly…I didn't trust me with me! I allowed others to have more of a say so regarding my existence. To the point where the ride had become so nauseating that I had to eventually make a decision. Unfortunately, or fortunately, depending upon the lens you have currently, the decision wouldn't come until much later.

Have you ever felt like you were on this constant roller coaster going nowhere? Are you clinging to a life that doesn't want you or one you have out-grown? If so, you are not alone. It wasn't until I had to make a decision between life or death. I was forced to choose from a life of security or living on purpose. Back in June of 2016, I was told that my position as the Associate Director of Leadership wasn't connected to teaching a course titled: *Foundations of Leadership* within the International Center for Studies in Creativity department at SUNY Buffalo State College. Now, I can imagine you're just as confused as I was. I couldn't for the life of me surmise the logic in this statement let alone the decision. All areas of my responsibilities were on par and in some cases exceeded my written performance program. Dare I mention how I wasn't even getting compensated for teaching the class. I mean really

 TAMARA L. MCMILLAN

had permanent appointment with New York State, making close to $80k annually and supporting my daughter through college as her custodial parent. If I was still holding on to a fixed mindset from my earlier years, I wouldn't have even considered the alternative. Having a growth-mindset is a healthy framing concerning your view of self. Carol Dweck has coined the phrase and her work is being used widely especially in the school systems. Dr. Dweck defines a growth-mindset in the following way "when people believe that their most basic abilities can be developed through dedication and hard work—brains and talent are just the starting point. This view creates a love of learning and a resilience that is essential for great accomplishment." I first came into contact with her work several years ago. As I was coming into a state of consciousness, moving myself closer and closer toward my own definition of personal freedom. I discovered her work through readings and conversations with others that also appreciate living a human existence of liberation. You see it's my strong belief that whatever we speak comes into existence. Words are real and once they leave our lips the universe conspires to give us what we asked for. A growth-mindset goes hand and hand with abundance and it protects the imagery we have of ourselves. An individual who operates from an abundant place doesn't see themselves as being fixed.

However, they may lack things in life, there maybe a lack of understanding for the subject of math. Recall the number of times you personally heard someone say "I'm not good at math". Does that number include you as well? I know I have personally claimed not being good at math more than a few times in my life. Why are all of these individuals holding on to the fixed idea that they're not good at something like math? Could it be because they have willing accepted an inferior position with the subject? Do they carry a fixed mindset because of their experiences years ago? Or do they hold a fixed mindset, because they haven't had the right tools for mastering the subject? The examples of why a person isn't good at something are endless. Perhaps, learning a new language is a tad bit more challenging than previously expected. Think about the number of times you got lost while driving in an unfamiliar city. The fact that you missed your exit isn't a sign that you're not smart enough to navigate a new city or that you can't get anything correct. It simply means you missed the exit. Just like learning a new job is arduous but it's necessary to accept a fixed mindset and declare never

 TAMARA L. MCMILLAN

applying for a promotion. Conducting your life from a fixed mindset is unhealthy and can be dangerous. Anytime something goes wrong a person with a fixed mindset will believe it has everything to do with their lack of intelligence and or abilities. They automatically think there's no way to fix these scenarios and acquiesce to a life of conformity and lack. The miscommunication with a boss during a meeting will be their sole problem to handle. The argument with a significant other will undoubtedly be their fault and cause them to feel uneasy about sharing their true feelings in the future. Causing the relationship to take a turn for the worse thus ending in divorce or two people living an expensive lie. Fortunately, with brilliant readings like Dr. Dweck's book, professional coaches, understanding self and this read offers examples of moving toward a growth mindset which is very attainable.

To close the circle on my personal example of how I used my growth mindset to live a life of ascension. The mere fact that the work of devising a plan using the creative problem-solving process wasn't enough. It really didn't matter how many damn good ideas my team and I had generated. The fact still remained that the heavy lift laid upon my shoulders.

How in the hell was I going to implement this plan? As this was the mother of all mothers, this was me placing my credentials and philosophy as an abundant leader on the line. Where everyone could witness my success or epic failure.

It is not the critic who counts; not the man who points out how the strong man stumbles, or where the doer of deeds could have done them better. The credit belongs to the man who is actually in the arena, whose face is marred by dust and sweat and blood; who strives valiantly; who errs, who comes short again and again, because there is no effort without error and shortcoming; but who does actually strive to do the deeds; who knows great enthusiasms, the great devotions; who spends himself in a worthy cause; who at the best knows in the end the triumph of high achievement, and who at the worst, if he fails, at least fails while daring greatly, so that his place shall never be with those cold and timid souls who neither know victory nor defeat.- Roosevelt

Instantly, I said there's nothing to lose but everything to gain. If I was going to bet on someone, I'd rather bet on me. Thus, project liberation was born. I sat down with my friend and editor to break down exactly how much income I would need to cover the house expenses, miscellaneous fees and incidentals. The number wasn't as large as I thought, especially since in preparation for the big leap I had already paid off all credit card bills. The largest and most significant bill I carried then and to this day is my mortgage. My old truck was paid off, my daughter was on scholarship with minimal bills and my school loan was just over one thousand dollars. After revisiting the numbers my growth mindset kicked into full throttle mode. I secured the bag by picking up three collegiate classes that fall, I interviewed and was hired to substitute teach for the Buffalo Public Schools and then I had my clients from my company to rely on. Wow, what a difference a day makes. Had I still held on to a fixed mindset, believing there would be no way for me to support myself, Jontay's last two years of college and keep the heat on, I would have capitulated too. Never acting upon the belief that I was worthy of something more. Destined to live the life I often daydream about each and every day. Fortunate for me, I was possessed with utter clarity of my life's purpose. Most successful people have a delusional quality about them.

They believe in what if, in what ways might I and they tend to dream big and in color. There are five things I know for sure:

1. I'm Jontay's mother
2. I was born to speak and teach
3. I'm an extravert
4. I'm passionate about education
5. I believe everyone has the right to live abundantly

These things made writing my resignation letter painless and effortless. I remember that day like it was yesterday. I didn't begin composing the letter until after 3pm on a Wednesday. There was not a doubt in my mind, I was beyond confident. I didn't call my mother or sisters. As a matter of fact, I didn't speak to any of my tribe members that day. The letter was short and to the point. To demonstrate what a letter from an individual who possess a growth mindset looks like, you can see the three sentences below.

13-July-2016

XXXXXX XXXXXXX

Director, xxxxx xxxxx Office

Buffalo State College

1300 Elmwood Avenue

Buffalo, New York 14222

Dear XXXX,

Please accept this letter as notice of my resignation from my position as Associate Director for Leadership. My last day of employment within the Student Life Office will be Friday, 12-August-2016.

I wish you and the office my very best!

Sincerely,

Tamara L. McMillan

This was paramount for me…I believe once you're clear on your Purpose…nothing or no one can corrupt that. She was the director and had a vision for my professional life that didn't align with my vision. There was no need at all under any circumstances to have this drag down knock out fight. It was her shop and I respected her position and opinion. Therefore, it wasn't necessary for me to convince her otherwise by pontificating. Life is entirely too short and I want us all to uncover our individual missions in life.

The two most important days of your life is the day you were born and the day you find out why.- Mark Twain

My friends…it's safe to say I found my why. But not without first asking myself…Who are you? This question was one that escaped me, or maybe I was afraid of what I thought was the obvious. Did I not want to look that lost, "inferior" black girl who grew up in poverty and fatherless in the face? At any rate, once I embraced my truth, my trials and missteps I refused to settle. It was time for me to put down the mask of social acceptance and continue working on mastering myself. Here, I uncovered the perfect space for self-awareness, self-acceptance and changed my perspective of me. Having a growth mindset offered me the opportunity to express my story authentically. I realized my story isn't just for me, it's for

 TAMARA L. MCMILLAN

all the bold, brave and brilliant beings I have and will come to know and love.

Vulnerability

Telling my story didn't come easy…I was under the impression that once I made peace with my past quietly… the work was done. It wasn't until I began serving in the role as mentor, sponsor and educator that my dirty little secret was out. I was being pulled and stretched in so many ways I couldn't take the uncomfortable feeling. I was being asked how I managed divorce, being a single parent, and was perceived as an unapproachable woman. At first this was a shock to my system. But when you're armed with knowledge, information and see the way we're all socialized and the ideology that feeds negative stereotyping it makes sense. Not that it's right but I am aware and it's the beauty and burden I carry as a black woman. On the contrary, my office suite is a revolving safe haven for young women and men who are eager for growth. The request to be a mentor, speaker, advisor and friend are constant. There was just one issue, I had yet to share all of me within my story. The more I became close to my constituents, the more they asked and the more I revealed. Surprised by the overwhelming reception, I was asked to go deeper and deeper. It was like a lightning bolt, eureka…it became clear on why I had returned to teach in higher education after resigning less than six months earlier. My vulnerability was a badge of honor and not something to hide. Sharing allows others to see your light and it gives them courage to be illuminated. I turned my failure and fear into (my) friend, all due to my growth mindset. I tell those that will listen, I'm a failure fanatic. You will read more about this phenomenon in the next step. During the first week of classes each semester, I tell my scholars the following and it becomes our mantra.

If you're not standing on the edge, you're taking up too much space.

My philosophy is…if I'm not failing then I'm not succeeding. Taking my growth mindset to the next level. Just like playing a video game, in order to grow and get better, you must play a formidable opponent as leveling up is required. I stand here unapologetic and authentic because I've been afforded the knowledge to master the language of growth. Being vulnerability is a notable experience as there's beauty in being vulnerable. Had I not been open and honest about my

 TAMARA L. MCMILLAN

fixed mindset, you and I may have never been afforded this unique exchange. You see we're all creative yet responsible for realizing our highest calling. Possessing a growth mindset is an amazing space to occupy, however, it doesn't relieve any of us from pain and struggle. Yes, the work will be rigorous. Yet, it will require us to declare who we are and why we were created.

Freedom

It's not complicated, when we allow ourselves to be curious about life, this invites questions. These very questions lead to an imaginative and growth mindset that offer options. Being free of a fixed mindset means I just don't have a few options at my fingertips. I have whatever I need when I need it. When we operate from a place of growth and self-mastery, we don't worry about protecting our "stuff". As growth advocates and creatives, we don't run out of ideas or ways to solve our problems. We lead from polarity…it's not this or that but this and that, as some problems are to be solved while others are meant to be managed.

My evolution has been a slow but productive journey. Hero's journey informs us that not everyone accepts their calling, as the walk through the dark, cold and wet cave is too frightening. Operating from an abundant/growth mindset, I know the universe is always at work for the good of all man-kind. Evolution is about finding multipliers in our lives. Those individuals that will take what we've created to a higher level. Just last month I received a text message from one of the scholars that took *Foundations of Leadership* with me the first semester I taught. She shared that she too now is teaching and wanted to let me know how grateful she was to have had me as an instructor and mentor. But more importantly, I'm appreciative that she was willing to allow me to play interference so she could follow her dreams. She and others like my graphic artist who began as an intern with me over six years ago are amazing examples of how the evolution process of a growth mindset works. When we share our gifts with others without expecting anything in return this brightens our frequency. Here is where true Freedom resides. For those of you who aren't connected to a growth mindset community or tribe, ask yourself "in what ways can I learn more?" My invitation to all of you reading this book,

  TAMARA L. MCMILLAN

especially if you're not living the life you deserve. In what ways might you begin changing your mindset? How many people in your immediate circle are standing in the gap and assisting you with growing? There are some reports that indicate by 2020, the state of New York will be a minority-majority. A growth mindset is too important not to share and experience. As we will need everyone at the table in order to develop the best team possible. This community of growth minded individuals are progressive, diverse and dedicated to building a world we can all be proud of. Living a life of abundance isn't this elusive, esoteric thing that's reserved for the special among us. Wouldn't it be great if we could all come along in an effort to finding our truth, voice and freedom? Moving us from a place of Knowing to Doing and finally Being. Because after all, what's Life without LIBERATION!

It is only in active self-expression and pursuit of
our own aims that we can become free.
-Brendon Burchard

Fear/Failure Fanatic

Our love for being right is best understood
as our fear for being wrong
-Kathryn Schulz

HOW MANY TIMES have you laid awake in bed unable to stop thinking about a dream that won't leave you? It's a reoccurring movie that plays repeatedly in your mind, and each time it ends you are riddled with questions. While at work, you spend hours' day-dreaming about the things you would rather be doing. You often do anything to avoid completing your required work. Social media is a welcomed escape from your work life of boredom, monotony and bureaucracy. The dreams are frequent which makes it more difficult to focus and be present. If you're able to identify with at least one of the above, you represent part of the 53% of Americans who dislike and or hate their jobs. You like them live for the weekends. And you're most definitely not thanking God it's Monday! Are you working in a position that doesn't fit your passions? Is it your plan to retire after 30-35 years with this company because you're playing it safe? Are you following the dreams and plans that others have crafted for you? I can recall listening to several scholars who I've had the opportunity to know on a personal level as a higher education professional and adjunct lecturer. If I had a dime for every time I've heard "I'm studying medicine because of my mother". Or "everyone in my family are lawyers", I would be filthy rich. Well, not so much filthy, but I would have amassed several hundred dimes during my tenure.

Are you too suffering in silence because you fear failing? Do you feel trapped by your familial responsibilities or the uncertainty of dancing to your own beat? Many of us take on the consumption of pleasing those around us by staying busy with minor tasks. As the thought of following our dreams instantly paralyzes the strongest among us. How often can you recall conceding your daily life with mindless distractions? Hypnotized by a false but compelling desire to respond to the needs of those around you. Pulled every which

TAMARA L. MCMILLAN

way but loose, we're often unsure of how to find balance between the needs of those we love and our own aspirations. Our busy work consumes all of our days but unfortunately, the work doesn't feed our life's purpose. Is your schedule more of a holding pattern instead of an action plan for your life? Are you serving in the role of victim or victor? Have you mastered saying no? No, is a complete sentence and needs to be used frequently, because there are those individuals who plague us and our mission. Is it your sister who calls to gossip about her mother-in-law? Or your ex-husband who has no friends and needs to hear himself talk. Their lives are not our responsibilities, we don't have to and shouldn't feel like we must save everyone. Think of being on an airplane during push-back, the flight attendant instructs all passengers to first place the oxygen mask on themselves before assisting anyone sitting next to them. We can't save anyone until we save ourselves by doing what we love. There's no denying our wide smiles and the quickening of our heartbeat when we imagine the life we deserve to live. One filled with happiness, power, true meaning and greater joy. This life awaits all, but it requires us to consciously choose. At times the mind rationalizes a million reasons why it would be too risky to start that business, write a book, go back to school or become a public speaker. Especially, since public speaking is feared more than death, so they say. I believe that it's not actual death that's feared, but the fear of being wrong. Many are fearful they won't do well on stage, some might think privately about forgetting the words or not connecting with the audience. This could be more about wanting to appear perfect and feeding the ego. Of course, we all want to do well in all that we do, but when we embrace the notion that nothing is perfect. It is then we can truly be free to express ourselves authentically without fear looming over our heads like a dark cloud. When fear isn't properly put in its place there is an enormous cost to be paid. We understand innately that fear exists everywhere and rules more than freedom. We know this to be true as the word fear shows up in the Bible 365 times, one for each day. Fear does more to draw us into its clutches and command the attention of scarcity. The voice is loud, harsh, unrelenting and unforgiving most times. Many of us never step out on faith to follow what we feel in our hearts, because of this powerful word. Fear has held too many hostage and for too long. Franklin D. Roosevelt reminds us

TAMARA L. MCMILLAN

Think of all the successful people you know, whether personally or otherwise. I invite each and every one of you to find at least one successful person that hasn't dealt with fear. I will go out on a limb and declare that it will be almost impossible to find anyone who hasn't feared something at least once. So, what would make us think we would be exempt from taming our own personal fears, especially as we chart a course of excellence? Oprah has shared many times with her millions of viewers how she was fired from one of her first jobs in television, because her boss determined she was too emotional. Just think being emotional is one of the many reasons why she has been so impactful and unstoppable in a variety of ways. Could you imagine if Oprah had listened to her former boss and began to compromise pieces of herself. Because of the fear of not being employable, what if she changed what she knew intuitively about her passions in life. Instead she decided to take the lessons learned from that situation and applied them to better her craft. Now, we all have the benefit of her authentic self, living the life she deserves to live and calling upon her right to be free of fear. Think of the Wright brothers and their obsessive quest to fly airplanes. They took all profits from their bike shop and dumped it into the research and development of their dream to fly airplanes. There were others at the same time attempting to do the same thing. One of their competitors had the backing of big businesses and all the support necessary to be the first to fly. The Wright brothers unbothered or intimidated by their competition, never took their eyes off of the larger picture. Did they have fears, of course they did. But the difference with them was they refused to allow fear to live rent free in their minds. Their ambitions and behaviors were larger and couldn't be constrained. As a matter of fact, they spoke to their fears by openly accepting to fail as a means to succeed. As they knew the more they failed the closer they would be to success. This step on fear…is tethered to embracing failure as a stepping stone to living the life you want and deserve to relish. It wasn't until I began really studying business women and men that I wondered what they possessed that made them successful in life. What were some of the attributes they held that separated them from the rest of the pack. I had to know, because living a life that wasn't designed for me is no longer an option. I know there is something more in life not only for me

 TAMARA L. MCMILLAN

but for you too. Life isn't meant to be lived feeling miserable, sad and hopeless. Now, dare I mention our 16th President of the United States? Abraham Lincoln was known as a bold and unrelenting intellectual. Yet, he too suffered great failures on an epic level. He lost his mother at an early age, then his high school sweetheart died, which almost caused him to experience a nervous breakdown. He was beaten numerous times in his pursuit of becoming a politician. Persistent, he stayed the course and ultimately ran and earned the highest position in these United States, Commander in Chief. The ultimate testament of him exercising his personal freedom and gawking fear in the face. He knew with certainty that if he followed through with his political agenda it could inevitably lead to his death. Well, since we all studied the history books, we know how his story ended.

If you're processing why I'm sharing stories you already know and have heard a billion times. Well, it's simple as my niece Kennedy would say. When you embrace that fear isn't your friend, it will then be necessary to tame this negative emotion. This will require you to be clear on the triggers that causes your fear to rear its ugly head. It could be an event that took place in high school, or the constant ridicule of your teachers and classmates. We can't forget those so-called loved ones who tears us down every chance they get. It's worth noting that a desperate person will do almost anything not to lose. Many would sabotage their success in order to prevent us from reaching our goals. They come off as concerned and caring, but their only concern is self. We can't trust a word they say and must be prepared for their undermining attacks. We must not be shocked when the rumors and hurtful criticisms begin, only to be followed by a fluctuating attitude. However, we must be steadfast in the pursuit of our own happiness and freedom. As a growth mindset leads to the doors of personal freedom. Fear can only win if we allow it to. Will you allow fear to roar louder than your impulses, desires, passion and dreams of being great? Think of the person who carries more weight than normal for their height but refuses to exercise because they fear not accomplishing their weight loss goals. What about the high school football player who wants to take dance lessons with his girlfriend but worries that his friends will tease him. Then there's the single mother who wants more for her life and often dreams of going back to school. However, the fear of not getting in or having to contend with traditional aged students stop

 TAMARA L. MCMILLAN

her from applying. Picture the insecure female athlete who is fearful of standing up for herself when her teammates try to undermine her personhood. Know this, if fear continues to rule the day, and our existence, it's because we've allowed it. Mediocrity is rampant yet excellence is rare. Ask yourself what's life without struggle? When we're able to ascend from the ashes, bloody and bruised from combat this serves as our indoctrination into a life of freedom, prosperity and winning. Joseph Campbell writes about struggle in the *Hero's Journey*. There are twelve steps that are divided into three phases. The calling, the separation and the return. The calling represents us receiving a nudge or whisper that connects us with our dreams and purpose in life. As you can image, there are too many to count who forgo their dreams because of some kind of fear. The idea of fear and foes are dealt with in the second phase, here is where one must differentiate who their allies are and enter the cave of darkness alone. As the journey can only be experienced unaccompanied. This strengthens our mindset and moves us from meek to motivated.

As an adjunct lecturer out of the International Center for Studies in Creativity, we use the coined term "trial and learn" often. When you open yourself up to the possibilities, that's exactly what comes into your world. Options will ultimately lead to freedom which serves as the cure to being fearful. Instead of asking "why me", I implore you to ask "why not me"? Thomas Edison is not only known for being the individual who first received the patent on the light bulb, he's known for the following quote:

"I didn't fail 700 times, I discovered
700 ways that wouldn't work".

I hope you're beginning to see the same patterns over and over again in some of the most successful people in the world. I'm also hopeful you will begin to see that fear is robbing you of a life worth mentioning. In this step, before moving to the next one, I encourage you to reflect on the things you fear, the feelings associated with that fear and finally see if you can acknowledge them as a part of your journey into a world free of fear and failure.

Before offering you the space to ponder your personal and professional fears and past failures that may have been associated with them. I first want to share some more fabric in supporting ways to approach eliminating fear. Most

   TAMARA L. MCMILLAN

of us hold on to fear because it's steeped in anxiety that's unfortunately amalgamated with two kinds of pain. We believe that if we make any changes or stand on the edge of greatness, the risk would be too arduous. Thus, we're bound to either lose something or someone or will endure some kind of hardship. Remember, the single mother who wants to return to school but she's holding on to the fear that she might not have the acumen to finish college. She questions whether she can keep up with the fast pace of college and students twenty years her junior. What about the person who wishes to lose some weight, but is concerned about what food options they would have available to them. Then the person who is being undervalued at work. Their egotistical boss doesn't offer any support nor allows them to use their natural talents within the organization. In addressing our fear and pain, we gain mastery over them. Like we discussed in step one, we can't master anything until we've mastered self! The words on these pages are here to encourage you to adopt an abundant or growth mindset. I'm wanting you to begin betting on yourself, the same way that Oprah, Michelle Obama and Steve Jobs did. Let's take notes from their books and life lessons and kick fear in the mouth. For the individual who isn't being supported at work, would begin looking at their glass as half full instead of half empty. They would no longer be concerned with losing their office space, having new colleagues or self-sabotaging thoughts about getting a new job. Rather, they would celebrate the opportunity to grow their network by meeting new people. They would welcome a new office space and a thriving work environment. The individual that is concerned with viable food options would see new restaurants and recipes as a refreshing alternative. They would visualize the feeling of walking the stairs without becoming winded. The single mother would see returning to school as a sign of strength and empowerment. Her example would be a highlight for her children especially her daughters. She would use her cultured life as a way to bridge the gap between herself and her young college classmates.

Some of us avoid seeking out the life and dreams we deserve because we think it will be too difficult to accomplish. We're often scared that we're not ready, capable or have the intelligence to make our dreams come true. Isn't it true that those who were able to experience great success didn't have all the answers either? The sheer joy and happiness of visualizing the life they warranted far exceeded their fears. They knew

   TAMARA L. MCMILLAN

their life's purpose was bigger than those small thoughts. Just imagine how awesome you would feel to openly welcome new perspectives and move toward those things that sparkle at you. Recall the number of times you wished for something different, a new way of existing and the pleasure associated with being able to stand in your truth honorably. At some point, your growth mentality will eventually begin to take over by reminding you that you're worthy of a better life and these small inconveniences are a part of the process. Affirming your individual process is another way of honoring your person. As worrying about the things that didn't work out as planned and living in the past won't change anything. Like the notion of crying over spilled milk won't change the fact that the milk is on the floor.

However, a step in any direction is better than standing still wasting time for the benefit of nothing. If a mistake is made, there's something called course correction. Meaning, we have the chance to evaluate the situation, assess what worked, and what we would change and why the next time around. Businesses no matter their market or focus, get plenty wrong. They spend hundreds of millions a year on advertising, product development, training and marketing etc. When their ideas don't work out the way they forecasted, do you think they just throw the whole planning module out the window? Hell no, my friend, they get back to the planning table to assess the analytics. Here, they determine the best ways to use what worked, modify what didn't and get rid of anything that doesn't fit. This would be no different for you and me, after analyzing the triggers surrounding our fear, we would address them by changing our perspective. When fear shows up it normally comes loaded with images to reinforce the positioning. Thus, in order to rid ourselves of these debilitating thoughts, the negative images must be replaced with another image, something positive. Eureka… Reframing requires a conscientious effort to be unflappable and will take some time to master. The more we become self-aware and accepting of a better life, the realization that there's more to gain than lose will be omnipresent. And following our dreams will outweigh the fear of not getting it right. For example, how many of you are familiar with WD-40? WD-40 is a 60-year company located in San Diego, California. The flagship product WD-40 is a lubricate that penetrates stuck parts and replaces their moisture. Many people may not know the meaning behind the name WD-40. The creator and developer of the product named it WD-40 because it took him 40 times to get the product consistency correct. Yes, you read that last sentence correctly…40 times! Ask yourself after failing at a task or while trying to create something you were passionate about, how many times did you try until you got it right? Did you fear that you would never get the right formula or combination of items to work for your project? When we secure the reframing approach and remain unmoved concerning any task at hand, this very process would inevitably produce more individuals living out their specific missions in life. They would be looking forward to each and every day instead of living for the weekend or dreading the notion of going home to a loveless house. However, if we don't make any advances in the direction of owning our life there's nothing to compensate for or reframe.

Take me for example, I didn't consider myself a fear/failure fanatic until two very significant things happened in my life. First, I was introduced to creative studies by my sister. She took a class on facilitation and swore she instantly thought of me and felt as though the training would be a complimentary piece to add on to my growing business model. When your sister, someone you value as a professional and knows she has your best interest at heart makes a suggestion more times than not we look into the idea. Well, I did what she suggested and she was unequivocally right. The training and the education as I often say saved my passion. It gave room for creatives to spread their wings, be their peculiar selves and most importantly, mistakes were welcomed. As a matter of fact, it's a pre-requisite to the education and a foundational aspect of what's used in the corporate setting during training and facilitation sessions. Imagine my excitement, a place where I can be free and they're delighted at the notion of mistakes. My advisor at the time gives all of his scholars at the undergraduate and graduate levels, mistakes quotas for each day during the academic semester. Ok, how fucking unorthodox is this? I'm used to an educational setting that is known for killing creativity and judging pupils based on the number of correct answers on a test. Here, I was now faced with a dilemma, how to shed the preconceived notion that the end goal was to be perfect. Was this true or was my professor trying to play my classmates and I. I and so many others are brainwashed into living out of fear, that we question the very things that make sense. It would be normal for one to make mistakes…right? Isn't it safe to say that as human beings we

 TAMARA L. MCMILLAN

wouldn't have the answers to every question posed to us? Just think how boring life and this world would be if we had all of the answers? Then I ask you, why is it that we're scared to death of making mistakes? Why does fear run our lives more than our passion and interests? It's incumbent that we make a decision. A decision to do what's required to be one with self and the universe. Make a decision and make it right!

Here are five ways **Resilience Experts use Fear/Failure to Succeed in life:**

1. Understand you aren't and will never be your Fears and failing is a door way to success. Most educational systems have brainwashed us in believing that failing is a bad thing. When our teachers, principals and administrators should have created an environment where true learning can happen. Meaning every student could be taught in ways that best supported their learning style. Ditto sheets would have been burned and more engaging and interactive experiences would have been in the place of the traditional model. Students wouldn't have been compared to one another

and all would have been called scholar. Thus, giving them the power to look fear in the eyes unscathed.

2. Failures are lessons of opportunities, when we're open to learning from them. Life has a way of giving us exactly what we need and when we need it. So, instead of looking at the things we so-called got wrong. We can view them as a trial to determine what can be learned. It's all about perspective. Changing the lens, we look through can invariably offer wild and crazy ideas we wouldn't have otherwise considered.

3. Free yourself and others of the stigma associated with fear and failing by sharing your mis-steps. I remember being told that I shouldn't share my fears, pain, heartaches or failures, because doing so would have placed me in a vulnerable position and I would be seen as weak and fragile. However, it wasn't until I began sharing some of my story with a few mentees, that I realized it was important. Telling my story and outlining the things that created fear in my life not only freed me but it became apparent that I was helping to free those around me. The more I shared, the more I was asked questions and this surprisingly

TAMARA L. MCMILLAN

liberated me. When we show those around us that it's normal to not have all of the answers and hitting a few bumps in the road is all a part of owning our personal responsibilities as a free soul.

4. Create a tribe to assist you in areas outside of your brilliance. No one person knows everything nor ascend to great heights alone. Think of any major position, someone who is successful on many levels… it doesn't matter if you're thinking Bill Gates, President Obama, or Hilary Rodman-Clinton. There are many things they have in common and one of those things are each and every one of them have a team. Or as I like to call it a "tribe". I have a tribe of individuals in my immediate circle who not only hold MEE up but they hold me accountable. They are brilliant in areas where I am not. Yes, I only surround myself with dynamic people who are smarter than me. They're on the cutting edge, the kind of innovation that's needed in order to win. Who's on your team? Are they telling you what you want to hear or are they making you and your mission better? Do they keep you on track when fear tries to rear its ugly head?

5. Make peace with the circumstances created by your fears. Be grateful for them and move forward. This step is one of my favorites but it's also one that's terribly difficult to accomplish. Once I've experienced a misstep, failure or a hardship, I acknowledge it. Then process what I believe the lesson is, forgive myself by hugging and kissing me and I release it into the universe. When fear tries to remind me of the error later, I quickly and confidently pull up my new positive image. While also reminding myself that I made peace with the incident. This is exactly why reframing is critical, remember fear won't go without a fight. Fear will scream, fight, scratch and pull on your emotions in order to stay in power. Your joy, passion and desire to live free of fear has to be stronger than the roar of fear. Period!

Think of it this way, successful people don't allow fear to paralyze them and neither should you. They intrinsically understand their dreams are worth following and nothing is more important than fulfilling their calling in life. Remember, there's only one thing worse than allowing fear to win and that's quitting! If you haven't already taken the time to ponder the questions about your fears, the feelings associated with them and how they play a role in your journey; this would be an ideal time to do so. As this exercise will be more beneficial for the content in the next step. Reflection without action is dead.

Resilience

Hurt is where you begin

-Anonymous

WE'VE MADE IT all the way to the second last step in our liberation now series. Relax your mind, release any unwanted energy from your being and the space you're in now. I would like you to take a few moments to breathe with your eyes opened. Now, take three to four deep breaths in and out with your eyes closed. Repeat as many times as you need before returning to this space. How do you feel? What did you notice about this quick meditative exercise? Were you able to clear your mind? Were there any thoughts that presented themselves to you? Or, were you able to just be still without any thoughts? I'm asking you these questions, as I've asked other questions along this journey.

Just like everything in this book, these very questions are intentional too. The world we live in is busy, noisy and filled with distractions that could lead to destruction. Many of us barrel through life wanting the pain to stop. We hardly make or find time to just be. Suddenly, we're self-medicating with any and everything that prevents us from handling said issues, challenges and mis-steps in life. We join another committee, start drinking, or turn a blind eye to the things that require our attention. This book will be published shortly after the New Year. One full year into the new administration taking office after eight years of President Obama serving as Commander in Chief. Regardless of who you voted for and yes, I'm taking the liberty to assume that each of you exercised your right. It goes without saying that in this last year we all had to be resilient. As you all know, I prefer offering a definition of the word that represents the step we're examining, as it gives us all the opportunity to be on the same page.

Without further ado, Webster's dictionary offers the following: *resilience is the ability to readily recover from an illness, depression, adversity or the like*. There's one word in that definition that immediately jumps out at me. Can anyone of

TAMARA L. MCMILLAN

you guess which word it is? I will give you a hint, it's not the leading word…resilience. I will give you a minute to re-read the definition and then before continuing, I would ask that you write the word along the left or right-hand side of this page. The previous step dealt with how fear keeps us from aiming high due to the anxiety associated with failing. If there's a possibility that we could fail, we readjust our goal by aiming lower. However, now that we spent time diving into fear, why it exists and ways to eliminate it from our psyche. This by no means suggest that we will be exempt of challenges, struggles and obstacles as individuals who are living a more conscious lifestyle. Now, for the word that jumped out at me in the definition of resilience. "Readily", how apropos for this step. We must be ready in a moment's notice to combat the naysayers around us. The very people who insist they have our best interest at heart. But their own goal in life is to suck out all the positivity in the world. Their sad existence is to play the role of victim and point out all of the things we've gotten wrong in life. They get up daily thinking of ways to lightly poke at us as we move towards those things that twinkle at us. One of the ways in which they make themselves feel better is by pulling us down with their ignorant and judgmental statements. Like the office colleague who insists on asking why you work so hard. Or the barrage of darts thrown by family members as you make the decision to leave an abusive relationship. I recall the comments I received from my great uncle about deciding to get a divorce. The relationship wasn't progressing and neither one of us was happy. Once my daughter was born, I began thinking about the messages I would be sending had I remained in a loveless, unhealthy and verbally abused environment. When my great-uncle approached me at a family cook-out sly as a fox. He asked me why did you leave your beautiful home in the suburbs with the attached garage to move back into your mother's house. Instantly, I was insulted and hot like fish grease. How could he ask me such a question? I'm his niece and it appears that his only concern was with the materialistic aspects of my failing marriage. Never mind that he's not spending time with me or nurturing our family. Hell, do I need to mention the infidelity, the lack of communication and camaraderie? During this strenuous time, I had to accept that I had made a huge mistake by getting married. We had very little in common and were more like roommates than husband and wife. Truth be told, we weren't even friends. The

 TAMARA L. MCMILLAN

list unfortunately was a bit long and we both played our part. Nonetheless, regardless of whose fault it was, this is where our wonderful word "readily" comes into play. Being resilient as someone interested in aiming for the stars will be critical. You can't allow the feeble minded, weak and unsure to rattle your confidence or question your life decisions the way my great uncle tried. I must admit, I didn't have a lot of respect for my great uncle as he too was a serial philanderer. Although he isn't with us any longer, that situation played a pivotal role in my new-found singleness. Had I not been secure in my decision his line of questioning could have shattered my budding confidence among other things. I could have seen returning to my mother's house with my daughter in tow as a step backwards.

The more I stood for myself, the more people turned out to cut up. When on my path for aiming high and making my dreams a realty, the weak, worriers and most definitely the wicked stopped at nothing to derail my plans. Please know these feelings aren't delusional. Like I did, you will ask yourself is it me? I questioned if I was the one whose was insane? The self-talk will increase, it will consume you if you're in the least bit unsure. It's important that you recognize and prepare for all of the emotions that will present themselves. You must be ready to defend your positioning in life, like I had to numerous times. You must be ready to safeguard your truth by way of being resilient. Being resolved isn't about convincing anyone that you're doing the right thing. It isn't about getting them to buy into the purpose and meaning of your existence. It is most definitely about you employing the art of not giving a fuck. This may seem harsh, cruel and insensitive, but, ask yourself what's the alternative. Have you heard of survival of the fittest? When you get questions like the following: Are you sure you want to do that? Do you think you will like that? Are you sure that's for you? Will you be okay living alone? Is owning a business really your dream? The questions and ridiculousness will be endless; thus, you will need to be headstrong and steadfast always. Remember, misery loves company and those that are weak, complacent and just down right wicked will stop at nothing to steal our bliss and courage. When these attacks come, we must stay the course and be resilient at all costs. The larger issue is those around us aren't strong enough to step out on faith, so they allow their paths to be controlled by fear. They aren't equipped with the resolve, patience and grit to command

 TAMARA L. MCMILLAN

their individual freedom. Which results in them playing the position of marionette. These are not the kind of examples we should be following, so let's stay on our path to bigger and better things in life. It's sad, but many operate out of a space of conformity. Look at our education system and why it was created. It was designed so society could have a bunch of cogs that would never question authority by cooperating and staying in their place. Seth Godin and Sir Ken Robinson have amazing TED talks where they explain how schools, and most institutions kill creativity and aren't interested in people living resilient and liberating lives. Seth asked his audience "what are schools for?" Passionately, he pronounced during his talk that schools were about teaching obedience and discipline. In my account, society isn't interested in grooming us for what we truly desire to do in life. Just think back to your elementary and high school days. What was the first thing you had to do once you got into class? If you were educated in a public-school system like I was, then you may have been responsible for completing bell or homeroom work. Think about how the desks were arranged, how different were the classrooms? Did you like the students today sit in rows, in an assigned seat looking at the back on someone's head for nine to ten months out of the year? Can you recall a time when you were celebrated for being unique in school? Do you have any recollection of being encouraged to be different and stand out? Can you imagine an instance during your primary school days where any and every idea you had was given a chance? Or were your ideas immediately judged and shot down like mines? It's a known fact that we're not taught to defer judgement, or be playful anymore; as if growing up was a form of punishment against having fun. The moment something is new and out of the box, we attack what we don't understand or can't comprehend. Was there ever a time where you felt motivated to seek wild and crazy ideas? Face it, we live in a society where conformity is celebrated and creativity is tolerated if mentioned at all. In the classroom teachers are still using ditto sheets for some lesson plans. The number of students in the classrooms are growing and resources are dwindling, making it even more difficult for learning and individuality to happen. How can we be expected to welcome our unique person by following our dreams when we haven't been given the freedom to be? Therefore, the idea of being resilient requires us to reprogram our thinking. We've become experts in collecting dots but have missed the mark when it

   TAMARA L. MCMILLAN

comes to connecting them. All significant occurrences in life aren't standalone occasions, they are meant to be used as a learning tool. Embracing our missteps is a way for us to look conformity in the eye and forge through adversity with no fear. As fitting in is a short-term strategy that will get us nowhere and standing out and being resilient produces results. Brendon Burchard in his award-winning book sums it up the best with the following statement:

"All their taunts and threats and terrors function to make us fear for our safety, security, or prosperity so that we might fall in line with their demands". With their demands of moving us away from our destiny in life. We all deserve to fully and completely experience the full expression of life without feeling stuck.

Unfortunately, out of know where, it happens again leaving us searching for some sort of explanation. Then the evitable becomes clearer as we then try to emerge from the fog, doing our very best to escape the murky thoughts of what now? What happens in life that causes us to feel trapped and stuck? Are we just moving along in life, mindlessly with no real intentions of pushing any envelopes or committing ourselves to stepping outside the lines to make a point?

What does being stuck look like? Where did this concept come from? Who was the ravishing individual that coined the term "I'm stuck"? When hearing and thinking about the word…stuck, what are some of the common images that come to mind? Well, if you're stuck, no pun intended, I took the liberty and Googled the word to see what my search would yield. The first three things that came up from the search were:

1. Stuck in love

2. Stuck in the middle and

3. Stuck on a feeling.

Now, your thoughts may have pictured a car's tires being stuck in snow if you reside in the north like me. Or was it an item being stuck in the ground or in concrete or someone's shoe getting stuck in the mud. Then there's the notion of being stuck in a dead-end job going nowhere fast. Where does the idea of being stuck originate from? Does being stuck look

     TAMARA L. MCMILLAN

the same for everyone and does everyone end up finding their way out of being stuck? There is a certain reality that many are very aware of regarding being stuck in a dead-end career. Unfortunately, not everyone has the passion, enthusiasm and will to be resilient in order to get unstuck. Sadly, too many people embrace this sad state of affairs and only live life after work hours and on the weekends. This is more than problematic, as life is full of wonderful surprises that await those that are true to themselves. Besides our weekends are extremely too short just to live happily three days out of seven. As the perceived walk of death called Monday morning is always lurking around the corner. Did you know the majority of heart attacks happen on Mondays?

Consequently, what are some things that those around us are doing to never get stuck? Or when they find themselves getting stuck, what tools and strategies are exercised for getting unstuck and on to bigger and better pastures? Those that I see who are able to get unstuck, are the ones that are fluid, flexible and most importantly resilient. They are the people who don't get bent out of shape at the sight of an issue and or challenge. They are the truth seekers that roll with the punches. It's understood that the world we live in isn't perfect therefore, they don't expect life to happen without a crisis. Simply put, these are the people who are willing to reinvent themselves through the practice of resiliency. In fact, they're eager to use any scenario as a starting point for a new chapter in their life. If there is a new position posting within their company, they are jumping at the opportunity. They are the individuals who stay connected to the movers and shakers at all costs. They are networking outside of their companies, and they are offering their assistance to colleagues in need. They constantly go where the opportunities of growth exist, even if that means packing their families up and relocating. They welcome celebrating the chance at getting better even at the cost of rejection! Resilience is that quality that can serve us all well if positioned at the right time for the right reasons.

Not all who wander are lost
-J.R.R. Tolkien

Cut from a different fabric, those that rarely stay stuck live by the creed of every time they get knocked down it's an opportunity to dust themselves off as they rise. Think of those in your circle, a family member, colleague, or neighbor.

 TAMARA L. MCMILLAN

It doesn't matter how arduous the situation, we can all be assured that they will come out on the other side fighting to the end. All things considered, this doesn't mean they win every race or land every job quest they engage in. What it does mean however, is that they use everything that's given to them. They take the lessons that are valuable and leverage them strategically for the next conquest.

There's a perfect public example we've all heard of and read about in this book. Most can relate to her in one way or another…Oprah Winfrey again. When she decided that it was time to do something outside of her talk show. She created her own magazine that adorns her face each and every month since its launch in April 2000. Next up, she wanted to give back on an even larger scale, so she built a school in South Africa for black girls only. If that wasn't enough, she developed and created her own television network called OWN. All things weren't coming up rosy for the billionaire superstar mogul. The network wasn't doing as well as everyone had anticipated to include Oprah. There were many articles, reports and skeptics all adding their two cents as a way to get to the bottom of the matter. Oprah didn't pack it up, and rest on her laurels. No Ma'am, she pulled out her resilience hat and went to work with her team. Revising, recalculating, reviewing and reconfiguring a new strategy for the network. They added, eliminated and partnered with key celebrates to boast the network into a space of prestige. She brought on heavy fitters like Tyler Perry, Iyanla Vanzant and Ava DuVernay to name a few. I use her story all the time, as she's a phenomenal example of an individual having a handle on her personal freedom, yet still enduring life challenges. If Oprah, Tyler Perry, 50 Cent, Shawn Carter, Steve Jobs and thousands more had to be resilient in their endeavors for liberation, why would we think we wouldn't need to do the same?

Adversity does not build character, it reveals it.
-James Lane Allen

Take me for example, I started my business in 2000, the main mission was to have an annual conference over a long weekend for women from all walks of life. The platform was about creating a wholistic environmemt where we could come to share our challenges, hurt, desires and pain without needing to censor our material. A place for women to lay their burdens down and just be without pretense. Well, that

     TAMARA L. MCMILLAN

conference never happen, I lost money, time, energy and most importantly my confidence. I was unsure if I was cut out to run my own business. I wondered if I had a viable product that people would pay for? The questions were daunting. But they weren't enough to stop me. Yeah, I was concerned and at times scared out of my mind. Resilience was the difference, when the conference didn't happen I took time to regroup. I did what big businesses do, I assessed. However, this time I created a dream team…MEE's board of directors. A brunch was set at my home and the invitations read regrets only. There were six accomplished, powerful and dynamic women who showed up to hear my pitch. The results, in less than one calendar year we successfully planned our first conference. The feedback was so great, we ended up hosting two more consecutively. The last conference was standing room only and chairs were added to accommodate our eager guests. Being clear on my purpose gave cause for my resilient attitude. I wasn't willing to concede to defeat and live a mediocre existence. Eighteen years later, I'm still growing and learning but I'm living the life I deserve to live. Through being resilient I am now a published author, an award winning speaker and lecturer who travels the world and most importantly I love my life!

Now, it's your turn, how will you get unstuck? How will you use the challenges of the day, week and month to reinvent yourself through being resilient? Life is a metamorphic process where we evolve and grow through our lessons. Just like a butterfly needing to be resilient in order to free itself from its cocoon. Welcome the new chapters in your life as an unexpected gift. Consider it a special wink and a smile from the universe.

Here are five ways to foster your own Resilience:

1. Nurture yourself- at times we forget about taking care of self. Take a day each week to relax, get a massage or my favorite...do nothing. This allows for work/life balance and ensures you're not driving yourself into the ground.

2. Identify your Purpose in Life- It's no secret that I'm big on purpose. I believe we all have a specific mission to complete in life. When we're crystal clear on what

TAMARA L. MCMILLAN

that task is, it's incumbent for us to begin leveraging that talent.

3. Embrace Change- In order for us to complete our individual mission in life, we must wrap our arms around change. It's okay to be comfortable, but nothing grows there. When we're open to change it allows room for us to connect with the world in a genuine and pure way.

4. Solve Problems- Increasing your ability to solve problems is critical in this day and age. Many collaborators, organizations and employers indicate that it's difficult to find people with creative problem-solving skills. Defer judgment when solving problems, reconnect with your playful side, don't rule out the wild and crazy ideas and make connections between unrelated things.

5. Commit- Once you've made a decision, make it right. Being resilient is all about staying with a task, when you're knocked down get back up. Work on building your resilience skills daily. Commit to being a life-long learner of you by being more aware.

Then use the strategies that best work for you personally and professionally. All in all, resilience takes time to build. Don't get discouraged about the small mis-steps in life. Use them as a training ground for getting ahead in life and allow them to serve their purpose. The walls of adversity don't exist to keep us out, they exist to determine how badly we want in. Enjoy the trials and learn from the experiences and get busy living a life free of societal constraints.

TAMARA L. MCMILLAN

Time: The Real MVP

Time is our most precious resource

-Brian Tracy

I CAN'T BELIEVE IT'S already 2018. Is it me or wasn't it just 2017? This book will be finished, published and we'll all be on to living a life of liberation. Looking forward to moving into 2019 with a new sense of purpose and a secure mindset of growth and self-acceptance. For me, time has truly been my go to when I must make a decision. In the past, I was always undercutting myself by just giving my time away. I remember with a frown on my face the number of times I waited for people. The times I sat hoping and wishing things could be better in my life. The ridiculous amounts of time I waited for a guy to pick me up only for him to show up hours late. That was one of the most unpleasant lessons for me. Now, when I have any kind of meeting or date, that individual has a twenty minute window, after that your gurl is out. I tell my scholars and daughter not to unwisely waste their time and never allow someone else to foolishly spend their time.

I'm going to share five things to consider when maximizing your own personal MVP...TIME! But before I give you these last items and send you on your way to begin living an abundantly liberated life. I would like to tell one last story. This story is yet again another tale of how I began taking all of my dots and started connecting them. I've been able to connect them to assist me with sorting out the issues I never addressed. With my education, performance coach and the practice of being deliberate, I have been able to make peace with and heal the internal upsets in my life.

As a girl I vividly remember when it was time for my sisters and me to go places with our mother, we would all race to the car. As it was our desire to sit in the front seat with her. It was as if the front seat was some kind of a magic carpet ride, where we would have her all to ourselves. Not caring about the fact that the other two siblings were just in the back seat. On our

 TAMARA L. MCMILLAN

trips to the super market, there was yet again another race. A race to see whose turn it was to push the shopping cart.

Clearly, our mother had to have some kind of system in determining who would ride in the front sit and then who would be responsible for pushing the shopping cart around the store. Unfortunately, in my eyes it never seemed to be my turn to do either. This theme would continue not only in my own household but also in other aspects of my life. It was never my turn to do the things I deemed important and or exciting. This notion really began to bother me personally, so much so that I began questioning when I did things. As I was convinced that my timing was all wrong! After making certain adjustments to when I did things…I was completely shocked and alarmed that nothing changed.

It wasn't until I embraced the possibility that timing wasn't my issue. All too often we find ourselves in particular places for unknown reasons. And just because it's our time, that doesn't mean it's our Turn! Life offers us many lessons to learn and waiting for our turn is definitely one of them. Because when we go out of turn, things aren't given the proper time to develop. Thus, we circumvent not only our timing but when it's actually our turn! So, instead of concentrating on when it will be your turn, rather enjoy the fact that it's your time!

Life begins at the end of your comfort zone
-N.D. Walsch

Like I promised you will find the final points for consideration as you move into a space that honors your person and life. Time like life has a way of being unforgiving. Please ensure that you make the most of your time, talents and treasurers. Remember, time is the real champion as it's the one thing we can Never get back! Spend it wisely my friends.

Finally, here are Five things to consider about your precious TIME:

1. If it doesn't get scheduled, it doesn't get done.
2. Quiet time is a must.
3. Make every day your masterpiece...as there's no such thing as giving 85% today and 115% tomorrow.
4. Don't waste it, moreover, don't allow others to waste it for you.
5. Time is your friend when used properly.

 TAMARA L. MCMILLAN

You should be approaching your busiest time of the year. Meaning, you should be focusing on you and the ways in which you can be your very best self. Don't allow your dreams to get caught in the shuffle, hustle and bustle of a life you don't want nor desire. Remember, one must work with time and not against it!

Time waits for no one
-Y. Tsutsui

You have everything you need to be the amazing creature you were born to be. Use this book, the exercises, notes and all of your pain, heartache, joy and desire for more as your driving force. Stop at nothing, be consistent, ask for help when needed, forgive yourself when mis-steps happen and always celebrate your wins! Living a liberated life is awaiting, you just have to take it. Remember, the dream comes free but the hustle is sold separately.

Printed and bound by PG in the USA